The Puppies of Blossom Meadow

The Puppies of Blossom Meadow

By Catherine Coe

Book 3:
Sprite Surprise

SCHOLASTIC

Published in the UK by Scholastic, 2022
1 London Bridge, London, SE1 9BA
Scholastic Ireland, 89E Lagan Road, Dublin Industrial Estate,
Glasnevin, Dublin, D11 HP5F

ISBN 978 1407 19868 2

A CIP catalogue record for this book
is available from the British Library.

Printed by CPI Group (UK) Ltd, Croydon, CR0 4YY

Paper made from wood grown in sustainable forests
and other controlled sources.

1 3 5 7 9 10 8 6 4 2

www.scholastic.co.uk

Blossom Meado

Primrose Pond

Badger Burrows

Dai
Ha

Poppy Place

The Great Hedge
Buttercup Bridge
Bluebell Grove
Sunflower Square
Lupin Lane
Blossom Brook
Violet Green
Honeysuckle Hill

Also by Catherine Coe

The Owls of Blossom Wood

A Magical Beginning
To the Rescue
Lost and Found
The Birthday Party
Save the Day
An Enchanted Wedding

The Unicorns of Blossom Wood

Believe in Magic
Festival Time
Storms and Rainbows
Best Friends

The Puppies of Blossom Meadow

Fairy Friends
Mischief and Magic
Sprite Surprise
Dandelion Dance

Lucky Bunnies

Sky's Surprise
Petal's Party

For Isabelle and Maeve xxx

Chapter 1

Hot, Hot, Hot

Hot sunshine shone down on Amber, Kayla and Erin as they followed Kayla's dad into Doggy Delight, the dog kennels where he worked. The three best friends were helping out during the school holidays.

Inside the door of the red-brick Victorian house, Erin wiped away the blonde bits of hair that had stuck to her forehead. "It's so hot today!" she said.

As Amber and Kayla nodded, a German shepherd in the hallway woofed.

"It looks as if Poppy agrees," Kayla said, patting her favourite dog on the head. Poppy's pink tongue was waggling even more than usual today.

Kayla's dad pinched the end of his nose. "Phew – I think it might be a good idea to give the dogs baths this morning! And as it's so warm, we can do it in the garden. Amber, Erin, Kayla, would you be able to go to the storeroom and find the doggy paddling p—"

"Yes!" the girls shouted before Kayla's dad had finished, and ran through the house and into the garden. They had a secret inside the storeroom, and they couldn't wait to get there.

"Hi, Matt, hi, Spot, hi, Rosie, hi, Jeff,"

Erin called to the dogs they passed. She had a brilliant memory, and already knew the name of every single one of the dogs staying at the kennels by heart.

Each of the dogs – a sausage dog, a French bulldog, a chihuahua and a greyhound – barked gently back, and the three friends grinned. They loved being here, no matter how much work it sometimes was. They

couldn't have pets at home because it wasn't allowed in their block of flats, so this was the next best thing!

They reached the shed at the end of the garden and entered the storeroom. Kayla and Erin ran straight towards a cupboard on the far wall, but Amber hung back.

"Shouldn't we get the doggy paddling pools out before we go to Blossom Meadow?" she said, pulling nervously on her long brown hair.

Erin frowned. "Don't be silly!" she yelled. "Now's our chance to use the magic collar!" She jumped up to find it on the top of the cupboard ... but she was shorter than her friends, and couldn't reach.

"I don't think Erin meant to shout at you – did you, Erin?" Kayla nudged her. "We would just really, *really* like to use the collar now..."

"Sorry, Amber," said Erin, her cheeks going red. "You weren't being silly and I shouldn't have shouted. It's just that no time passes when we're in Blossom Meadow, remember? So when we get back we'll be able to fetch the paddling pools, and Kayla's dad won't know the difference!"

Amber's brown eyes widened. "Of course. I was worrying over nothing, just like my mum always says I do!" She jumped up and down, pointing to the cupboard. "Quick, get the collar then..."

Kayla leapt up to grab it, her black topknots bouncing around. She brought it down and the girls stared at the purple collar in Kayla's hands, which sparkled brightly in the sunshine streaming through the storeroom window. The shiny silver name tag swung on its chain like a pendulum clock, and the word Blossom blurred as it moved back and forth.

Erin and Amber reached out so that all three girls were holding the collar. Then they held their breath…

The next moment, white sparkles began spinning off the collar, whizzing around them like a hurricane. "Don't let go!" Erin squealed, as her feet lifted off the floor. The three friends rose higher and higher, and the storeroom disappeared in the cloud of sparkles.

Amber closed her eyes, just as she always did. It felt somehow safer that way! Her skin tingled with magic, like she'd been covered in popping candy, and her ears seemed to crackle with electricity.

Magic rushed around them, zipping and glittering, raising them ever higher… But soon Kayla felt solid ground beneath her legs again. "You can open your eyes now,"

she said to Amber softly.

"We're back, we're back!" shouted Erin. She spun around and stared down at her furry golden legs and paws – for every time the friends arrived in Blossom Meadow, they were no longer girls, but puppies!

Erin finally stopped spinning to look at Kayla and Amber, who were now a fluffy

brown cockapoo and a sleek black terrier. Erin was a cute golden Labrador, with big floppy ears and a very waggly tail. They were standing by the emerald-green water of Primrose Pond, which was encircled with pretty little flowers in yellow, red, pink, purple and orange.

Kayla scooped her head down to put on the Blossom collar for safekeeping, and felt wet all of a sudden. "Oh no, it's raining!" she said, shaking out her fur.

Kayla shook herself too, then looked up at the sky. "But there aren't any clouds – it's just as hot here as it is at home."

A frown crossed Erin's golden forehead. "So where is the rain coming from?"

"I don't know," Amber replied. "But let's get under that tree before we get soaked!"

They scampered to the nearest tree – a tall, wide oak with giant bright-green leaves. Kayla tilted her head and listened. "That's weird. It isn't raining here. I can't hear any raindrops on the leaves at all."

Amber pointed a black paw across to Primrose Pond. "It's only raining over there, look!"

Sure enough, they could see water was only falling at the edge of the pond. It glistened in the sunshine as it spattered down on to the primroses.

Erin leapt up and beckoned to her friends. "Come on – let's go over there and find out what's going on!"

Chapter 2

Water Fight

The three puppies were soon soaked again as they neared the pond. The water just kept on falling, and Erin, Kayla and Amber looked around, trying to see where it was coming from. They shivered with the cold water, and their fur dripped as if they'd been in a bath!

"Gotcha!" a squeaky voice suddenly cried.

A turquoise face popped up from the green pond and the water finally stopped falling.

Amber, Kayla and Erin stared at the creature while shaking out their fur, sending droplets flying everywhere.

"Are you a fairy?" Erin asked, taking in her pointy ears and delicate features.

The creature somersaulted out of the pond then, landing right in front of the puppies. "A fairy?" she yelped. "Are you joking?" She spun on the spot and the puppies could see she didn't have any wings – but fins at her waist and long webbed feet. "I'm a water sprite! Wilma's my name."

Wilma skipped around the puppies, stroking their fur as she went. "Anyway, what are *you*? I've never seen anyone like *you* around here! Are you from outer space? No, wait – I know. You're in fancy dress. Am I right? You're probably badgers or foxes,

coming to play a joke. Or on the way to a party!"

Kayla giggled. "We're not dressed up – we're dogs!" she explained. "Well, puppies, really. I'm Kayla, and this is Erin and Amber."

Wilma tilted her head to one side and her green flowing hair drifted downwards, almost touching the ground. "Oh! I don't think I've ever heard of *puppies*. But it's great to meet you, all the same. Welcome to Primrose Pond!"

The water sprite dived back into the water and for a moment the puppies thought she'd disappeared for good. But then it started raining again! They scampered to the edge of the pond and saw what Wilma was doing...

She had her face just under the surface, with her mouth open and her cheeks full. She was blowing the water upwards and spraying it everywhere. That was why it felt as if it was raining!

"Hey, Wilma!" Another water sprite leapt up from the other side of the pond and began flipping the surface with her fins, creating arcs of water that sprayed right across to Wilma ... and the puppies. The sprite didn't seem to notice that the water was going everywhere – or didn't care.

The three best friends shivered and shook themselves dry. They scampered a few steps back as more water sprites appeared and quickly joined in, sending water flying all around the pond. The creatures yelped and squealed and laughed as they created the biggest water fight Kayla, Erin and Amber had ever seen.

The puppies kept on walking backwards, trying to get away from the water.

"I don't like this!" Amber said.

"Come on, let's go," Kayla barked, and

her friends quickly nodded.

But just as they reached the big oak tree, they heard a shout. "Wait! Don't leave!"

The puppies turned around and saw Wilma was out of the water again, beckoning them over. The water fight was

still going on ferociously behind her. Wilma spun around and yelled to the other water sprites, "Stop a minute! I'm trying to talk to the puppies!"

Like a tap being turned off, the water suddenly stopped flying. Kayla, Amber and Erin padded tentatively towards Wilma, across the now soaking-wet grass.

Kayla twitched her little brown button-like nose. "We thought you were busy," she said, and pointed a paw at the pond. "You know, with the other water sprites."

"It looks like fun!" Erin added. "But we wanted to dry off a bit!"

Wilma bit her lip. "Will you stay now that we've stopped playing? I don't want you to leave – no one seems to come near the pond any more. It gets boring when it's just us water sprites all the time."

"Okay!" Amber said, feeling sorry for the water sprite.

Wilma flapped her fins in delight. "Great! I'd love to show you where we live – want to come and look?"

"Underwater?" said Erin nervously. Although she'd had swimming lessons at school, she wasn't sure how well she could swim as a puppy – and they'd get soaked again if they went into the pond.

But Wilma was shaking her head and smiling. Kayla noticed how much her eyes twinkled when she was happy. "You can look from the edge of the pond," she told them in her squeaky voice. "Come on, let me show you…"

Wilma beckoned them closer, then took a running dive into the pond. It was so smooth, it didn't create even one splash, just a ripple of circles that spread out across the emerald water.

The next moment, her head appeared and she swam over to the side of the pond where the puppies stood. "This is where we have all our meals," she said, pointing to a ledge of rocks below the surface.

Amber's eyes adjusted to the water and soon she could see it clearly – a big long rock, like a dining table with smaller rocks dotted all around it.

Wilma ducked under the water and appeared to the right of them, and the puppies followed her. "This is our garden – we grow all our own food to eat! Water parsley, water chestnuts, basil mint, lotus flowers..."

Kayla licked her lips. It sounded delicious and reminded her it had been hours since breakfast.

"Want some?" Wilma asked. A handful of water chestnuts came flying out of the water and the puppies had to duck to avoid getting hit.

"Ummm, thanks," Kayla said as she stuck

her snout into the wet grass to pluck one out. She munched down on it, and the rich salty flavour filled her mouth.

Wilma swam further around the pond. "This is where we sleep," she said, pointing at a bed of grasses dotted with pretty white flowers. Then she somersaulted into the centre. "If you look very carefully, you might be able to see our meeting place."

She dived down and Erin followed her white splashing trail with her eyes. She could just about make out a ring of rocks on the bottom of the pond.

With a whoosh, Wilma shot upward out of the pond. "Did you see it?" she asked, in mid-air. "Of course, we don't have a lot of serious meetings. Mostly they're about how we can have more fun!" Wilma hit the water again and her head bobbed up, her face filled with a smile. "So do you like it?"

Kayla nodded quickly. “Oh yes, it’s beautiful!” she said.

“But I think we’d better go now,” Amber said quietly and looked at her two friends. “You know … we’ve got that thing we must do…”

Erin frowned at Amber. “What thing?”

“I’ll tell you in a moment,” Amber whispered, as she pulled Kayla and Erin away from the pond. “It was lovely to meet you,” Amber called over to Wilma. “See you soon!”

“Oh, okay!” Wilma squeaked, waving a turquoise hand. “But do come back again soon!”

Chapter 3

Missing Creatures

Amber only slowed down to a stop when they were well away from Primrose Pond. Ahead of them, Violet Green spread out like a thick purple carpet.

"What was all that about?" Erin asked, putting her paws on her hips. "Why did we have to leave so suddenly?"

"I think I know why no one goes to Primrose Pond any more," Amber said as she bounced up and down on the spot. "The water sprites are too annoying!"

Kayla nodded, making her fluffy brown ears jiggle. "You're right," she said. "I mean, it's pretty clear they just want to have fun, but I don't think they know when to stop..."

Now Erin nodded too. "It's a bit like when my little brother wants to play with my toys. He's only trying to have fun, but he sometimes messes everything up and then I don't want him anywhere near me!"

"But what can we do?" Amber barked.

Kayla shrugged and her little brown tail dropped. "I don't think there's much we can do. We probably shouldn't interfere too much in what's going on here. We're only just getting to know Blossom Meadow."

"But if we see the water sprites again, we can try to tell them!" Erin said.

"I'm not sure I'm brave enough to do that," Amber replied.

Erin grinned. "Don't worry. I will!"

"Hey, look, there's Buttercup Bridge," said Kayla, pointing a paw across Violet Green. "Let's go over and see the fairies." They'd met the fairies on their first ever visit to Blossom Meadow, when they'd helped them save their bluebell home.

"Good idea!" said Erin, already bounding towards the bridge that was dotted with bright yellow buttercups at both ends. She slowed down as she reached the bridge,

treading carefully over the pretty flowers that were like a pillow under her paws. As she stepped across the wooden bridge, she looked over the left side, and then the right. "Trudge? Trim?" she barked, hoping to say hi to the trolls that lived underneath it.

"The trolls aren't here?" asked Amber, as she and Kayla caught Erin up.

Erin shook her head. "I can't see them anywhere!"

"I guess it's better than when Trudge was making everyone who wanted to cross the bridge give him something…" said Kayla.

It had been a tricky problem to solve, until the puppies had realized Trudge was only doing it because he was unhappy.

"That's true!" said Amber, remembering how upset the other creatures in Blossom Meadow had been.

Erin began running again, turning her golden head back to Kayla and Amber as she reached the other side of the bridge.

"Come on," she called. "Let's find the fairies!"

The puppies ran along Lupin Lane, between the tall, beautiful flowers in red, pink and purple, then swerved off to the left towards Bluebell Grove.

There was no sign of any of the fairies. *Maybe they are behind the bluebell grasses*, Erin thought. They were quite shy creatures, after all.

"Where are the fairies?" Amber asked

as she caught up with Erin yet again. "Hello?" she called out gently.

But all they could hear was the rustling of the grass in the gentle breeze. Kayla arrived, panting, her pink tongue waggling. "Phew! It's too hot to keep running like this. Maybe we should go back to the pond and have a water fight to cool down!"

But Amber wasn't really listening to Kayla. She had her nose to the ground and her ears pricked to the sky. "Bran? Sen?" she said, repeating their fairy friends' names over and over. Finally she lifted her head and shook it. "I really don't think they're here," Amber said to her friends.

"So what do we do now?" Erin sighed.

Kayla frowned, screwing up her little black eyes. "It's a bit strange that the trolls weren't at home, and now the fairies too. Where do you think everyone is?"

The puppies were quiet for a moment, then heard the whizz of wings above. They looked up to see a butterfly with white wings and purple tips zooming towards them.

"Chloe!" Erin shouted, waving her paws up to get the butterfly's attention. Chloe was the first creature they'd met in Blossom Meadow, but they hadn't spent much time with her, as she was always fluttering about in a rush.

The butterfly grinned and shot down towards them, stopping suddenly just above their heads. "Oooh, hello, puppies! It's ever so nice to see you back again! But I can't stop – I'm on my way to a Meadow Meeting in Sunflower Square."

That must be where everyone else is, thought Amber.

Chloe began flying upward again when Erin yelped, "Can we come?"

"Please?" added Kayla.

Chloe tilted her head and smiled. "Of

course! You're a part of Blossom Meadow now too. Follow me!"

The friends beamed at each other and began scampering after Chloe, their tails wagging like windscreen wipers. Luckily the sunflowers were right beside Bluebell Grove, so they didn't have to run far.

They reached the huge patch of sunflowers, the stalks almost as high as trees. Kayla kept her eyes on Chloe, but it wasn't easy now the sky was obscured by big round sunflower heads.

"Here we are!" announced Chloe, just as the puppies arrived in a square-shaped clearing in the middle of the sunflowers. Lots of animals were there, as well as the trolls. The puppies scampered in to find a place to sit.

Amber pointed upward, realizing the fairies were amongst the birds, butterflies and insects flapping their wings lightly in the sky above.

"Ahem. Ahem. AHEM!" came a voice, and the murmuring of the creatures died down.

Erin sat up to see who was speaking, and realized a badger was standing right in the centre of the square, on a tall yellow mushroom. She nudged Kayla and Amber, who followed her gaze and smiled. The badger was George, another friend of theirs. It seemed he was in charge of the Meadow Meeting!

As the square became silent, George held up a clipboard and started to read in his growling voice.

"Welcome to today's Meadow Meeting. We have a couple of brief announcements to

begin with, as follows… Due to the recent lack of rain, the water level in Blossom Brook is very low. So please no diving into the brook unless you want a broken limb." George glanced up from his clipboard. "Foxes, I'm looking at you…"

The puppies searched around the crowd and spotted a skulk of foxes in the middle, whose faces had all flushed red.

"I also want to remind everyone about the annual Blossom Banquet," George went on, "which is taking place next week. If you want to enter the Dandelion Dance competition, don't forget to give your entry form to Edna Mouse."

A banquet and a dance competition? thought Erin. She really hoped they'd be here for that!

"And now for the main topic of today." George sighed and then continued in a sad

Chapter 4

The Meadow Meeting

George beckoned to a nearby bird, which had black feathers and a bright white beak. "Charlie, would you like to come and speak?"

The bird waddled up to the yellow toadstool. As George slipped off it, Charlie hopped on. He looked about the crowd for a moment, and then opened his beak to talk.

"My family used to spend a lot of time at Primrose Pond," Charlie said in a squawk. "But lately, the water sprites are just too much. They're always playing pranks! And I'm sure it isn't just us coots that are affected, right?"

The puppies looked around the square and saw a lot of nodding heads and flapping wings. A toad raised her hand and Charlie waved at her to come to the toadstool.

She leapt from her spot in the crowd to

the top of the toadstool in just one jump, and the coot had to fly quickly upwards to avoid a crash.

"Hello, everyone," she croaked deeply. "Now, I really don't like to moan, but I'm at the end of my tether with the water sprites. They keep stealing our water lilies, so we have nowhere to sit. Sometimes they even take one when we're sitting on it. Right from under our feet! I know it's just a joke, but they don't seem to know when to stop."

Many of the creatures in the crowd gasped as the toad told her story.

"I say we boycott Primrose Pond completely," the toad went on, her voice so low it seemed to come right from her belly. "Maybe then the water sprites will stop playing pranks. After all, they'll have no one to play them on!" She turned to

George, nodded, then leapt off the toadstool.

George lumbered back on and addressed the crowd once more. "So there we have it," he said. "It sounds as if we should put it to a vote. All those in favour of avoiding Primrose Pond, raise your paw, hand or wing..."

There was a loud rustle across the square as creatures moved their limbs to vote. When Amber looked around, she saw everyone had put a hand – or wing or paw – up. *Should I put up a paw too?* she

wondered. But she wasn't sure she agreed, so she didn't move and just hoped no one would notice.

George clapped his big black paws together. "I don't think we need to discuss it any further. It's clear we're all in agreement. No one will go to Primrose Pond." He glanced at his clipboard. "That seems to be all for today. Meadow Meeting dismissed!"

The animals, birds, insects and creatures chittered and chattered as everyone began

leaving Sunflower Square.

Erin turned to her two best friends in alarm, her eyes as big as chestnuts. "But they can't just stop going there," she whispered. "The water sprites don't realize how much they've upset everyone!"

"You're right," Kayla replied. "Blossom Meadow might be divided for ever!"

Amber's ears shook with worry. "But what do we do? We can't even go to the pond to explain everything to them…"

The puppies fell silent and hung their heads. When Kayla looked up, she saw that they were all alone in Sunflower Square. She gazed at the collar around Amber's neck, which would take them home whenever they chose. "Maybe we should go back home?" she said.

"No, we can't do that!" Erin shook her head hard. "We have to try to fix this!"

"Well, we could get as close to the pond as we dare," Amber suggested. "Maybe we can shout loud enough to get the water sprites' attention?"

"Good idea," said Kayla. "I don't really want

to go home yet!"

The puppies jumped up and began running out of the sunflowers, along Lupin Lane and across Buttercup Bridge. The trolls were sitting beside the bridge on the riverbank, wearing their usual brown dungarees and long, laced shoes. They smiled as the puppies passed them, tipping their large grey heads. Erin, Kayla and Amber waved, but they didn't stop. All they could think about was getting back to the pond. Or as close as they could without actually being *at* the pond, anyway…

After scampering across Violet Green, they reached the oak trees around Primrose Pond.

"I really don't think we can go any closer," said Amber, worrying that they'd be spotted by someone and get into trouble.

Kayla put a paw on a tree trunk and peered around it towards the pond. "All right then – let's shout from here."

"Wilma!" the three puppies called out, as loudly as they dared. "Wilma! Are you there?"

Amber and Kayla stopped shouting to listen for a reply, but Erin kept going. "Wilma! WILMA!"

"Shh," Kayla said to Erin as kindly as she could. "We can't hear whether or not Wilma is calling back if we just keep on shouting."

Erin smiled sheepishly and fell silent. The three puppies pricked up their ears as high as they could, but there was no sound of the water sprites – only the buzz of nearby bees and the distant flap of butterfly wings.

Amber breathed in and sighed deeply. "They must be underwater. They wouldn't be able to hear us from there…"

Erin poked her head out from the tree, searching the pond for any sign of the water sprites. "We can't even see them!" she said. "If only we could fly, and then we could try waving at them from the air…"

"But we can ask someone who can," Kayla replied. "Fly, I mean! And isn't that Chloe up there?"

They didn't even have to shout to get Chloe's attention. She must have spotted them from the sky, and was already shooting down towards the puppies.

"Ooooh, are you playing hide and seek?" Chloe asked as she zoomed closer and came to land on the lowest tree branch. "Can I join in?"

"Um … not exactly," Amber said.

"We're … um…"

"We're trying to speak to the water sprites!" Erin finished for her. "I know we're not supposed to, but they don't know how much they've upset everyone. We thought they needed to know, and then they might change!"

Kayla raised herself up on to her hind legs so her nose was level with the pretty butterfly. "We didn't want to go against what everyone agreed, but we didn't know what else to do."

Chloe's wings stopped mid-flap. Amber wondered if this meant she was thinking. The puppies waited for her to say something, but she stayed silent.

"Are you okay?" Erin asked when she couldn't wait any longer. "Will you help us?"

"Pardon?" said Chloe. She blinked as if she was waking from a deep sleep. "Oooh, yes, I'm fine. Just needed to rest my wings for a moment. How do you mean, help you?"

"Can you fly above Primrose Pond and see if you can see the water sprites?" Kayla asked.

Chloe fluttered her wings. "I guess… But I don't want to get too close to the pond. We agreed at the meeting we wouldn't. Besides, the last time I flew too low, they splashed me so hard I nearly spun to the ground!"

"Thank you," Amber said as Chloe shot upward and over to the pond. The puppies watched from behind the tree as she flew across the water and circled around the circumference a couple of times. Then she began to head back.

"I can't see anything," Chloe told them as she landed on Erin's shoulder. "I'm sorry."

"It's okay," Erin said, smiling at the

friendly butterfly. "You tried your best. Thank you."

Chloe nodded and then tapped a foot. "I've got to go, I'm afraid – I was on my way to Butterfly Ballet when I saw you. Good luck!" And with that, she leapt off Erin's shoulder and whirled into the air, soon just a dot in the bright blue sky.

As Amber watched Chloe go, her heart sank to her paws. What would they do now?

Chapter 5

Acorns!

Amber and Kayla looked at each other, all out of ideas. Meanwhile, Erin had moved away from them, and had her head down low towards the grass.

"What are you doing, Erin?" Kayla asked.

Now Erin's snout was pressed to the ground, and she was snuffling into the

grass like a piglet.

Erin snuffled a little more, then flipped her head up. "Immmm fndddd orns," she said.

"Um, pardon?" said Amber, unable to understand anything Erin had just said.

Erin opened her mouth, and three large acorns fell from it. "I'm finding acorns!" she repeated.

"Okaaaay … but why?" Kayla asked.

Erin glanced over towards Primrose Pond. "We can throw them into the water to get the water sprites' attention. That way, we don't have to get too close."

"Great idea!" Amber said, and started searching the grass for acorns too. After a few minutes, the three friends had collected more acorns than they could carry in their paws.

"Amber, I think you should throw them," Kayla suggested. "You're the best at sports. I'm not sure my throw would even get them to the pond!"

Amber sniffed with alarm, but Erin nodded. "Kayla's right," she barked. "You're brilliant at rounders and throwing the ball to the bases!"

"All right," Amber said slowly. She *did* love playing sports. But this seemed much more serious than games at school…

The puppies dropped their acorns into a pile by Amber's paws. She took aim with the first one, lifting her paw and raising it above her head. The acorn made a perfect arc in the sky as it shot towards the pond and landed right in the centre with a *plop*!

Kayla clapped her brown paws together. "Great shot, Amber. Can you do it again?"

"I think so..." Amber's little pink tongue stuck out as she lifted a second acorn and aimed it at the pond. It hit the water in the exact same spot as before.

"You're so good at this!" said Erin, passing Amber another acorn.

Amber kept going – throwing acorn after acorn into the pond. If the water sprites were in there, this would definitely get their attention! *Come on, Wilma*, she thought. *Where are you?*

She reached down to pick up the last acorn from the pile, and heard a shout. Actually, not one shout – lots of shouts. Amber looked up and smiled. There were the water sprites, leaping out of the pond.

The smile quickly fell from her furry face. The water sprites looked furious!

"Who's throwing things at us?" one of them yelped. "You won't get away with this!"

"Quick, hide!" said Erin, scampering behind a tree. Amber and Kayla followed her, but the water sprites were heading right for them, sprinting across the grass and dripping water as they went.

The puppies ran to another tree further away, hiding behind the trunk. "Maybe

it wasn't a good idea to get the sprites' attention," Kayla half-joked in a whisper.

The water sprites were amongst the trees now, spreading out as they searched. Amber could see Wilma headed exactly in their direction. "I shouldn't have thrown the acorns," she said. "It's my fault."

"No, it's not," Kayla whispered back. "We told you to do it!"

Erin peeped around the tree, took a deep breath and yelped, "It was us!" She jumped out from behind the trunk and waved her paws in the air.

Wilma squealed in surprise and skidded to a stop, the fins at her waist shuddering. "What? Huh? Why did you…?" She trailed off. "I mean … puppies, it was you?"

The other water sprites ran over to join Wilma, pond water still dripping from their hair and fins, making the tiniest pattering sounds on the grass.

Erin pulled a face and nodded.

"But … I thought you were our friends," Wilma squeaked. "Do you hate us like everyone else does?"

"No!" Kayla said quickly, scrambling out from behind the tree to join Erin. "We don't hate you – and neither do the other creatures in Blossom Meadow. But we do know why no one comes to Primrose Pond any more."

"You do?" Wilma squealed, her voice even higher than usual.

"Yes. You see everyone else … they're…" Kayla didn't quite know how to say it.

"They're fed up with your pranks!" Erin said for her friend. "They've had enough of all the games and tricks – even if you were just having fun. So they agreed that no one should come to the pond, and then you'd have no one to play your pranks on but yourselves!"

No one said anything for a moment. Amber took a step back, worrying that this revelation would only make the water sprites angrier.

Wilma looked around at the others, sighed and put a turquoise hand to her mouth. "And that's why you were throwing the acorns!" Wilma said. "You couldn't come too close, but you wanted to tell us."

"Exactly," Kayla barked. "We really didn't mean to upset you."

"Just like we didn't mean to upset the other creatures," Wilma said, her voice full of sadness. "And now they're going to leave us alone for ever!" She burst into tears, picking up an oak leaf from the

ground and wiping at her eyes.

Erin looked at the other water sprites and realized that they all had tears in their eyes. *Maybe we shouldn't have said anything*, she thought. But it was too late now. She noticed Amber bouncing from paw to paw. "What is it?" Erin asked her.

"I think I have an idea," Amber said quietly, patting her eyes with her paws.

She hated seeing anyone crying – and the poor water sprites looked *so* upset. She took a deep breath, smiled and said to them, "But we'll need your help..."

Chapter 6

Sprite Surprise

"I really hope this works," Amber whispered to Erin and Kayla as they walked across Buttercup Bridge. The puppies were leading all the creatures of Blossom Meadow from Sunflower Square – where they'd just had another Meadow Meeting – to Primrose Pond.

They'd had to persuade George to hold a special meeting just a couple of hours after the last one. But he was a kind and helpful badger, who told them that the puppies were just as much a part of the meadow as the other creatures. So if they wanted a meeting, they would have one. That was the

way it worked in Blossom Meadow. Kayla wished their world back home could be just as fair!

At the meeting, the puppies had told the Blossom Meadow residents that they had a special surprise, and asked everyone to trust them. But as they drew closer to Primrose Pond, the creatures behind them began murmuring amongst themselves.

"Why are we *here*?" said a little red ladybird, who was flying just at the back of the puppies' heads.

"Yes, what are we doing?" buzzed a bee. "I thought we were staying away from the pond. The sprites are bound to play another prank on all of us!"

Amber looked at Erin and Kayla as they walked. They were smiling and didn't appear worried, but Amber was. What if the sprites didn't keep to their word? What if they did play more pranks? Then everything would get even worse!

As they reached the oak trees that surrounded the pond, Chloe flew up beside them. "Are you sure this is a good idea? I mean, I do trust you puppies, really I do, but I *don't* trust those water sprites! Why are we here? Maybe we should turn back?"

"It's okay," Kayla said, although her voice had the tiniest shake to it, as if she was nervous. "We mustn't turn back now." She let Chloe land on her shoulder and nestled the butterfly into her neck.

At the head of the train, the puppies walked through the line of the trees and out into the open.

"Where are they?" said Erin in a hiss.

"I don't know!" Amber whispered back, bouncing from paw to paw as they came to a stop at the edge of the pond.

Kayla looked back and saw that the animals, insects and other creatures that had followed them were keeping their distance, most staying close to the oak trees and some even hiding behind them.

"Puppies?" came George's growling voice. He emerged from the trees and strode up to the three best friends slowly, panting slightly from the long walk. "What is happening? May I ask why we're here, when we agreed to boycott Primrose Pond?"

"Um … It's just…" Amber didn't know what to say as George looked at her with his big eyes.

Erin ran right up to the edge of the pond and peered in, leaning so far over she got her golden ears wet. *Come on, water sprites!* She shook her head impatiently and was about to dip a paw into the pond when she heard a sound over the mumbling of the meadow creatures behind her.

It was light and delicate, a bit like someone singing. The next moment, the centre of the pond began to ripple, circles spreading out in waves from the middle. Then something popped out from the water – not with a splash, but with the gentlest shimmer…

A water sprite with long, wavy green hair emerged from the pond, a flute in her hands. She played into it as she rose from the water, until it seemed as if she was standing on the surface! When Erin looked closely, she saw that other sprites were lifting her feet below the water, batting their fins to keep the first

water sprite steady.

She stopped playing the flute and nodded down into the pond, waving her arms towards the water. The creatures watching her edged a little closer to the pond, and those that could fly zoomed upward.

Kayla gasped as she saw what was happening beneath the surface of Primrose Pond. It was full of the water sprites – and they seemed to be dancing to the flute! They held hands in circles, kicking their legs and somersaulting in time with each other.

It's like synchronized swimming, but better! thought Amber, who remembered watching the sport on TV during the last big tournament. Her little black tail began tapping on the ground in time to the flute's music. Her plan was working – so far!

Everyone gasped as the flute crescendoed and the sprites leapt up out of the water as one, spun in a mid-air somersault and then dived back down into the pond – all the while still holding hands and smiling. By now, the creatures of Blossom Meadow were crowded around the pond edge, all trying to get as close as possible to the dancing. The bigger animals, like the foxes and the badgers, lifted up the smaller animals like the caterpillars and the mice, so that everyone had a good view of the performance.

"It's beautiful!" squealed Chloe, still on

Kayla's shoulder.

Kayla grinned without looking away from the dancing water sprites. "They wanted to show everyone that they can do nice things too," she explained.

"This is better than nice." Chloe tapped her tiny butterfly wings in delight. "It's magical! And there hasn't been a single splash!"

The water sprites swam together as the flautist played the final notes of the song and then lowered back into the water, right in the centre of the creatures.

Everyone began clapping and hooting and cheering while gazing into the water, wondering if the water sprites would come back. Just as the applause started to die away, dozens of water sprites popped up above the surface of the water.

"We're so sorry!" squeaked Wilma, as she treaded water towards the right side of the pond. "And we hope our dance makes up a little bit for upsetting you. We do love pranks, but not as much as we like all of you – our neighbours. We promise we'll stop our tricks … and we'd love for you to start visiting Primrose Pond again. What do you say?"

The crowd burst into another round of applause. "I think that means yes," said George, beaming.

But Kayla had noticed something. "The water sprites look really sad," she whispered to Erin and Amber. "It seems a shame they have to stop having fun completely."

Amber rubbed her nose with a paw. "Maybe they don't have to!" she said, another idea springing into her head.

"What do you mean?" asked George, who might not have been the youngest Blossom Meadower, but his hearing was as good as anyone's.

"What if the water sprites get to play pranks around the pond on just one day of the week?" Amber suggested.

"Oh yes!" barked Erin, her little golden tail wagging. "Then they can still have fun, but without annoying anyone who doesn't want to be pranked."

Kayla nodded. "Because everyone likes a prank sometimes!" she said. "Life would be very boring without any jokes at all."

Now everyone clapped again, louder even than before. In the pond, the water sprites beamed from ear to ear.

"Thank you so much," called Wilma. She jumped out of the water and ran over to give the puppies a hug, followed closely by the rest of the water sprites. Erin, Amber and Kayla got wet as the creatures dripped water over their furry faces, but they didn't really

mind. What mattered was that everyone in the meadow was happy again – the water sprites included.

As the water sprites returned to the pond and the animals began drifting off, the puppies realized they should probably be getting home too. They found a quiet place behind one of the oak trees and Kayla tugged the magic collar off her neck so that all three of them could hold it in their paws.

As soon as they touched it together, the collar trembled in their grip, and they felt themselves rising up into the air. Purple sparkles zipped around them, so thick that they couldn't see anything except the bright, firework-like colours.

"Woohoo!" shouted Erin as she felt the magic surrounding her. And then they began to drop downwards, and the sparkles fell away, revealing the storeroom of Doggy Delight.

"That was another amazing adventure," breathed Amber as she landed on the ground, no longer a puppy but a girl once more. "I'm so happy we could help the water sprites."

"And now it's time for another adventure." Kayla grinned, picked up a doggy paddling pool and winked at her two best friends. "We'd better get ready to get wet again!"

Word Search

Can you find the words related to the sprites in this word search?

W	I	L	M	A	B	D	B	J	U
H	F	D	E	R	I	P	P	L	E
G	C	G	W	F	H	K	E	S	P
M	V	I	K	G	J	P	D	G	L
A	N	M	F	N	B	R	T	F	L
U	U	O	H	O	D	A	N	C	E
I	E	A	P	F	V	N	G	W	Y
H	C	R	I	Q	J	K	R	N	V
A	E	U	K	P	A	S	Q	S	T
M	B	B	L	S	P	L	A	S	H

 WILMA  RIPPLE  PRANKS

 SPLASH  DANCE

You can find the answers at the back of the book.

Erin Fact File

Want to get to know Erin better? Here are some fun facts about her. . .

Name: Erin Berg

Age: 9

Family: Lives with her mum, dad and sister, Phoebe

Favourite dog: Chihuahua

Transforms into: Labrador

Favourite hobby: Dancing

Favourite book: *Moon Dog* by Jane Elson

Likes: Meeting new people

Dislikes: Being quiet

Did You Know?

Butterflies taste with their feet!

A group of badgers is called a clan.

The girls look after all kinds of dogs at Doggy Delight – but did you know that there are almost 360 different breeds of dog in the world?

Although Erin doesn't like getting splashed in the book, Labradors LOVE water – in fact their tails are often called "otter tails" and their feet are webbed to help them swim better.

Making a Splash

Can you find the sprites in Primrose Pond?

(Follow the lines A, B, C, D)

You can find the answers at the back of the book.

Spot the Difference

Can you spot five things that are different in these pictures?

You can find the answers at the back of the book.

Meet

The Owls of Blossom Wood

in these magical books

Meet

The Unicorns of Blossom Wood

in these magical books

Meet

The Puppies of Blossom Meadow

in these magical books

Catherine Coe
The Puppies of Blossom Meadow
Fairy Friends

Catherine Coe
The Puppies of Blossom Meadow
Mischief and Magic

Read on for a sneak peek of
the fourth book in the series!

Chapter 1

Busy Blossom Meadow

"Girls, are you in there?" Kayla's dad called from the garden.

"Oh no," said Kayla. "Quick!" Inside the storeroom, she thrust out the purple dog collar so that her two best friends, Erin and Amber, could grab it. The collar shimmered, the silver Blossom name tag spun, and tingles zipped up their arms as the magic began to take hold. White sparkles circled around them, like they were in the middle of a mini tornado.

Amber squealed and shut her eyes. This bit was always the weirdest. It felt incredible to be wrapped up in warm, glittering magic – but it also made her panic a little, especially when her feet lifted off the floor.

"Are you OK in there?" came Kayla's dad's voice, closer now.

"He's going to come in!" yelped Erin as the white sparkles became a thick spinning cloud around them. "What if he sees us disappear?"

But they couldn't see the storeroom any more, and Kayla hoped that meant her dad wouldn't be able to see *them* either. He would get a huge shock if he did! At least no time would pass at home while they were away, so hopefully her dad wouldn't

miss them.

The next second, Amber felt her feet touch the ground. She opened her eyes slowly and saw the sparkles fading away. They were no longer in the storeroom of Doggy Delight, the dog kennels where Kayla's dad worked, and where they'd been helping out. Instead, they were standing among long grasses and green bushes dotted with white flowers. A rich, sweet smell filled the friends' nostrils. This was Honeysuckle Hill in Blossom Meadow. And their sense of smell was much better than normal, because they were no longer girls, but puppies!

"What's going on?" Erin barked, jumping up on her hind legs and looking around. Erin was a golden Labrador, with a shiny almost-white coat and a little wagging tail. Amber was a sleek black terrier, with a white tummy and perky black ears. And

Kayla was a chestnut-brown cockapoo, with super-curly fur and a panting pink tongue.

The friends looked on in surprise. They'd never seen Blossom Meadow so busy before – it was alive with creatures moving this way and that, both on the ground and in the sky. Bright butterflies swooped across the sky among buzzing bees and gliding birds. Animals ran across the meadow as far as the eye could see – foxes and badgers and mice and rabbits, squirrels and frogs and moles and deer.

Kayla waved at a passing hedgehog. "Excuse me..." she began to say.

The spiky hedgehog turned his head as he plodded through the grass. "I'm sorry, I can't stop. Too much to do!" And he kept on shuffling along. Kayla wondered whether to run beside him – he wasn't walking very fast – but decided that would be too rude

when he was clearly busy.

Meanwhile, Erin was trying to get the attention of one of the birds flying above. She leapt up and down, waving her paws. "Hello! Hello! Please come and talk to us!"

"No time!" twittered a blackbird. "Got to rush!"

"What's happening here?" wondered Amber, bouncing from paw to paw. "I hope there isn't something wrong."

The puppies had helped out with problems in the meadow before. Last time they'd been here, they'd helped reunite the meadowers when the water sprites had played too many pranks on everyone. Before that, they'd helped the trolls and the fairies. Erin, Kayla and Amber couldn't believe that they were friends with magical creatures as well as animals, birds and insects. It was a dream come true! They loved being in Blossom

Meadow more than anywhere else, which is why they'd been so relieved to finally have an excuse to get to the storeroom in Doggy Delight at the end of the day. Kayla's dad had asked them to return the grooming accessories to the shelf before they left.

But we only just made it, thought Kayla, as she scooped up the purple Blossom collar from the ground and on to her neck for safe-keeping. The collar was usually kept in the storeroom at Doggy Delight – they'd found it on top of a cupboard the very first day they'd helped out at the kennels. It was how they got to Blossom Meadow, and how they got home too, so they needed to take care of it! All they had to do was hold it at the same time, and it magically transported them there and back.

"Let's go and find George," Amber suggested, pointing a black paw in the direction of Badger Burrows. "If he's at home, he'll be able to tell us."

The three puppies scampered away across the beautiful honeysuckles, leaving their sweet scent behind as they ran on to Daisy Heath. They tried not to stomp on any of

the tiny white daisies as they gambolled over the grass – but it wasn't too difficult as there weren't many daisies growing there today.

Is that what's wrong? Erin wondered. *Have the flowers started disappearing?*

A large area of dry brown soil spread out

in front of them and they raced across to the hole that led to George's home. It wasn't the prettiest part of Blossom Meadow, but *inside* George's burrow was a different story. Erin poked her head into the entrance, which was lined with yellow and orange flowers. "George, are you there?" she called.

"Puppies, is that you?" a low voice replied. "Oh, do come in!"

The three best friends shuffled inside, one by one. As always, every available space in George's home was filled with bright bunches of flowers. Amber was relieved not to see any bluebells – they'd recently helped make sure the fairies' home in Bluebell Grove was protected by persuading all the creatures in Blossom Meadow not to pick the slow-growing flowers.

The puppies jumped up on to three tree-trunk seats around George's large log dining table. It was piled so high with flower garlands, the puppies could barely see over them.

"They're for tonight. Do you like them?" George asked, clapping his paws together.

"What's happening tonight?" Erin asked at the same time as Amber said, "Yes, they're lovely!"

George beamed. "Why, it's the Blossom Banquet! I thought that was why you were here. You are coming, aren't you?"

"So that's why everyone's so busy," Kayla said, her curly brown tail wagging in relief.

There was nothing wrong after all! "Yes, we'd love to come," she added, "if we're invited?"

George slapped a leathery paw on the dining table, making the garlands bounce. "Of course you are! You're just as much a part of Blossom Meadow as anybody. Now, have you entered the Dandelion Dance yet? There's isn't much time left before the noon deadline!"

Erin's golden ears pricked up. She remembered George mentioning the dance competition the last time they'd been in Blossom Meadow. "Oh yes, we'd love to," she said.

George waved them towards the burrow entrance. "Then as much as I'd love you to stay for elevenses, you'd better go and find Edna Mouse. She lives in the sycamore tree at the very end of Lupin Lane."

The puppies said goodbye to George and quickly left the burrow. They had to hurry – Lupin Lane was all the way past Violet Green and over Buttercup Bridge. They ran as fast as their legs would carry them. Amber wasn't sure she'd ever quite get used to running as a puppy, but it was fun all the same, galloping along and feeling the soft ground beneath each of her four paws. She was on the school athletics team, and wondered if she was faster at running as a puppy than as a girl.

They scampered off the bridge and turned right on to Lupin Lane. Kayla pointed out the sycamore right at the end. She raced out in front, running between the rows of towering purple and pink flowers that grew either side. The puppies soon arrived at the base of the gnarly tree trunk. It was the only tree around, so they knew this had to be the one. They were doubly sure when a little white face peeped out of a hole near the bottom.

"Are you here to register for the Dandelion Dance?" the mouse squeaked. "You're just in time!"

"Yes!" barked Erin. "I'm Erin, and this is Kayla and Amber." She turned to her friends, and realized she hadn't actually asked them if they wanted to dance in the competition. But luckily they were grinning – they were used to Erin's quick decisions, and they liked to dance

just as much as she did.

Edna wrote their names down on the tiniest clipboard they had ever seen. "Wonderful!" she squeaked. "We've never had puppies in the Dandelion Dance before. See you tonight, and good luck!"

"Thank you, Edna," Amber called as they left the sycamore tree. Then she looked at Kayla and Erin. "What are we going to do for the dance?" Deep down Amber felt a bit nervous about dancing in front of everyone. "We haven't danced together for ages!"

"Don't worry," Erin replied. "We have the whole afternoon to practise!"

Kayla nodded, making her fluffy brown ears bounce. "Come on, let's go and find somewhere quiet."

But they didn't get very far. Halfway along Lupin Lane, they heard tiny voices calling to them. When they turned around, they saw the blue figures of two fairies hovering in the air.

"Bran and Sen!" said Amber as she saw the fairy twins. "Are you all right?"

The fairies' faces were wrinkled with worry. "Not really," Sen replied as they came to land. "We were wondering if you might be able to help..."

Answer Sheet:

W	I	L	M	A	B	D	B	J	U
H	F	D	E	R	I	P	P	L	E
G	C	G	W	F	H	K	E	S	P
M	V	I	K	G	J	P	D	G	L
A	N	M	F	N	B	R	T	F	L
U	U	O	H	O	D	A	N	C	E
I	E	A	P	F	V	N	G	W	Y
H	C	R	I	Q	J	K	R	N	V
A	E	U	K	P	A	S	Q	S	T
M	B	B	L	S	P	L	A	S	H

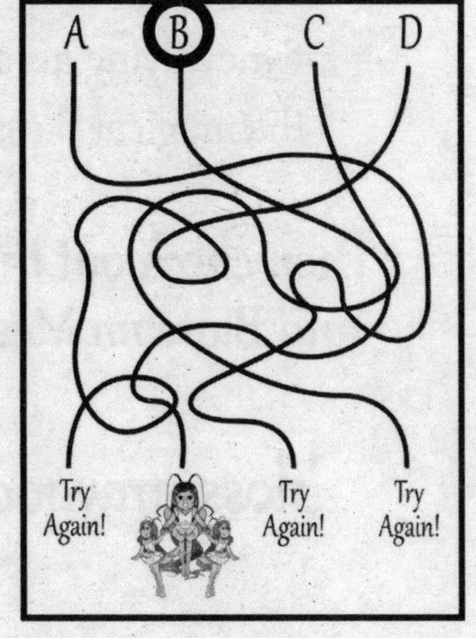

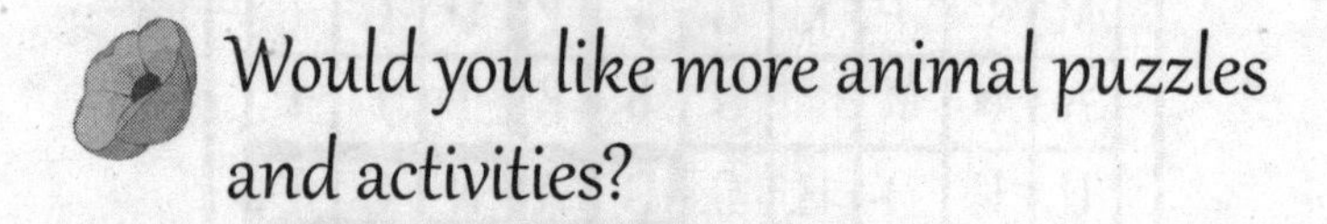

- Would you like more animal puzzles and activities?

- Want sneak peeks of other books in the series, including the Owls and Unicorns of Blossom Wood?

- Fancy flying across the treetops in the magical Blossom Wood game?

Then check out the Blossom Wood and Blossom Meadow website at:

blossomwoodbooks.com